MOONSTICK

The Seasons of the Sioux

BY EVE BUNTING

PAINTINGS BY JOHN SANDFORD

Joanna Cotler Books
An Imprint of HarperCollinsPublishers

Moon of the Birth of Calves

When the snows of winter disappear
my father cuts a moon-counting stick
that he keeps in our tipi.
At the rising of the first moon
he makes a notch in it.
"A new beginning for the young buffalo,"
he says.
"And for us."
Everything is new.
The trees bud.
The box elders run thick with sap
that we lick for its sweetness,
the sweetness of spring coming.

Moon of the Thunderstorms

Thunder rolls with the voice of many drums.
Light sweeps the cloudy sky.
It is time to move
to higher ground.
There will be game to hunt.
Our own animals will grow fat.

Strawberry Moon

My mother and my sisters
the aunts and the grandmothers
sit in the sunshine
and make leggings and moccasins
and paint pictures
on our new robes and parfleches.

The strawberries hide,
red as blood in their dark-green beds.
We put them in our deerskin bags.
The dog and the travois wait.

Moon of the Ripe Juneberries

A black bear may be there before us
when we go gathering
in the berry patch.
We surprise him and scare him away.
My mother pounds the fruit to mush
that we eat from bowls,
our fingers purple as bear paws,
though we have spoons.

Cherry-Ripening Moon

The men dance the Sun Dance.
I am too young to dance
or to hunt
as my father and my brothers and uncles do.
I am too young for many things.

Moon of the Ripening Plums

Before the hunt
the women sing their strong-heart songs,
the men smoke the sacred pipe.
"Mother Earth is generous
with her gifts," my father says.
"We take or offend."

When the men hunt deer they wear
the wolf-skin disguise
and go barefoot.
Deer have sharp ears
and it is good luck
to leave the moccasins behind.

Moon of the Yellow Leaves

The sky is endless.
The stars burn bright.
Today the hunters brought back
two buffalo.
"All animals are sacred,"
my father says.
"But the creatures that swim
or walk or fly
were put on the plains
that the Sioux might eat."
We share the fresh meat
with the Great Spirit
in thanks for the kill.

Moon of the Falling Leaves

The branches of the trees
are sharp as buffalo bones.
The leaves fly like golden birds,
golden, red and brown.
My father caught a crow
by its legs
when he was rabbit hunting.
He brought it back for me.
I will make a stick cage
and teach the crow to speak my name.

Moon of the Hairless Calves

It is sad
when hunters find calves
still unborn
inside the buffalo cows.
But my father says
a life cannot be without sadness,
buffalo or Sioux.

Moon of the Frost on the Tipi

There are fires in the firepits
inside the tipis.
The tipis glow orange
and people shadows dance on the walls.
Now my father wears wooden snowshoes
when he hunts.
Soon I will be old enough to go.

Tree-Popping Moon

Frost splits the wood
with the sound of thunder.
Wolves call.
My mother wraps my buffalo robe
close about me.
I am remembering how my eldest brother
trapped an eagle
at the time of the Strawberry Moon.
I will be as clever.

Sore-Eyes Moon

The sky is white.
The earth is white.
The rivers are white.
It is wise to look with care
or we will be sightless forever.

"Do not despair," my father says.
"Changes come and will come again.
It is so arranged."

Moon When the Grass Comes Up

It is so arranged.
The snows have melted,
the rivers opened.
Mother Earth stretches after her sleep.
Larks sing.
"One time follows another
on life's counting stick," my father says.
"When this moon dies
I will cut a fresh moonstick
and we will start again."

Many moons have died.
Many winters have passed.
My father is with the Great Spirit.
The buffalo have gone
and the eagles are few in the sky.

Our lives are different now.
My eldest brother works in a barbershop.
His hair is white as winter snows.
My wife does beadwork
and I make headdresses of feathers
that sell well.
We do not hunt.

Tonight is the night of
Moon of the Birth of Calves.
I will go as my father went
and cut a moon-counting stick
to keep in my house by my bed.
I will go with my grandson.
To him I will say,
"Do not despair.
One time follows another
on life's counting stick.
Changes come and will come again."
I was told once
that it is so arranged.

For the Sioux, the year began in spring when the hard winter was over.
They kept track of time's passing by counting the
thirteen moons, naming them according to the
signs of nature around them, their own
activities, or the food that was available
to them. One way to "number the moons"
was to make nicks in a moon-counting
stick, which was cut and kept for that
purpose.

For Glenn—E.B.

The author wishes to thank Richard Buchen, Photo Archives,
Southwest Museum, Los Angeles, California.

". . . in sunshine or in shadow"
For brother Dan—J.S.

The artist wishes to thank Ray Winters for his help and heart in the making of this book.
To the Sioux Indian Museum in Rapid City, South Dakota, and the Eiteljorg Museum in
Indianapolis, Indiana, for their patience, resources and generosity: everlasting gratitude.

Moonstick   Text copyright © 1997 by Edward D. Bunting and Anne E. Bunting,
Trustees of the Edward D. Bunting and Anne E. Bunting Family Trust   Illustrations copyright © 1997 by John Sandford
Manufactured in China. All rights reserved.

Library of Congress Cataloging-in-Publication Data
Bumting, Eve, date
   Moonstick / by Eve Bunting ; paintings by John Sandford   p.   cm.   "Joanna Cotler Books"
   Summary: A young Dakota Indian boy describes the changes that come both in nature and in the life of his people with each
new moon of the Sioux year.
ISBN 0-06-024804-1. — ISBN 0-06-024805-X (lib. bdg.) — ISBN 0-06-443619-5 (pbk.)
   1. Dakota Indians—Juvenile Fiction.   [I. Dakota Indians—Fiction.   2. Indians of North America—Fiction.   3. Moon—Fiction.
4. Seasons—Fiction.]   I. Sandford, John, ill.   II. Title.
PZ7.B91527Moo   1997   95-44865
[E]—dc20   CIP
                                                                                                 AC

❖
Visit us on the World Wide Web!
http://www.harperchildrens.com